My Parents Divorced Me!

Africa Hann

authorHOUSE®

AuthorHouse™
1663 Liberty Drive
Bloomington, IN 47403
www.authorhouse.com
Phone: 1 (800) 839-8640

Published by AuthorHouse   09/22/2015

ISBN: 978-1-5049-5034-3 (sc)
ISBN: 978-1-5049-5033-6 (e)

Print information available on the last page.

This book is printed on acid-free paper.

This Book is dedicated to
Dijionnaria Hann because she inspired
me to write it, Tia Patrick, Andre and
Jare Elam, Salena Gomez, and all other
children that have experienced the hurt of
their parents going through a divorce.

Divorce isn't such a tragedy. A tragedy is
staying in an unhappy marriage, teaching
your children the wrong things about
love. Nobody ever died of divorce.
-----------Jennifer Weiner, Fly Away Home

Chapter

1

It was the first day of middle school and all the children were standing around outside of the building laughing and playing, while waiting on the bell to ring, so that everyone could go inside of the building to eat breakfast in the cafeteria. The bell ranged; Ding! Ding! Ding! And the all of the children ran happily and full of energy to the buffet line. Suddenly a whistle sounds and a deep voice yelled out calm down children!

Calm down! It was the voice of Mr. Pringly the cafeteria monitor and at once there was silence in the cafeteria.

"Hello children my name is Mr. Pringly and I am the cafeteria monitor here at W.G. Wesley Middle School. This is my cafeteria and I will not tolerate any running, screaming, pushing, fighting, or jumping in the lunch line. There will be absolutely no food fights! I expect for each and every one of you to form a single filed line when getting your food trays, there will be no exceptions. If there is any horse play you will be pulled from the line and put out of my cafeteria. Now did I make myself clear and do we all understand?"

The kids all yelled out at once *"yes Mr. Pringly!"* Mr. Pringly went on to say… *"In my cafeteria we can all get along if you follow those simple rules, now that will be all and I hope that your first day of middle school will be full of excitement and fun, however educational. Now you may all eat your breakfast bone a petite!"*

The children started to talk amongst themselves, but quietly. The girls all gathered at one table and all the boys gathered at a separate table. Across the room there sat this one kid that stood out from the rest of the children in the cafeteria mainly because she sat alone at a table by a window. Once the girls noticed her they started to whisper, then one of the girls asked as she pointed her finger: *"who's that girl over there and why is she sitting alone?" "I'm going over to introduce myself."* Another girl replied.

As she walked over to the table she looked back at her peers as if she was afraid, however she finally built up the nerves to approach the other girl. *"Hello my name is Kelly, Kelly Johnson, what's your name?"* Kelly asked, the girl replied *"Zoe, Zoe Jones." "Nice to meet you Zoe may I sit down?"* Kelly asked. Zoe continued to look out of the window then she replied *"you can if you want to this isn't my table I'm just sitting here."* Kelly looked at Zoe and took a seat.

"So Zoe, what grade are you in?" Kelly asked. *"I'm in the sixth grade"* Zoe responded, *"so am I"* Kelly replied. Ding! Ding! Ding! The school bell begins to ring. *"Well it's time for class maybe I will see you around Zoe"* said Kelly. Zoe responded *"yeah maybe you will Kelly goodbye."* As the bell rang all the kids ran out of the cafeteria and off to class, the hallways were suddenly empty. Zoe entered her classroom and took a seat. *"Hello six graders, my name is Mrs. Jefferson and I'm your six grade English, homeroom and physical education teacher, and I look forward to an exciting and fun, however educational school year with all of you. Now before we get started I will do a roll call, when you hear your name being called I want you to respond by saying present, is that understood?"* *"Yes Mrs. Jefferson!"* The children yelled out.

Mrs. Jefferson began the roll call. *"Tonya Amis."* *"Present!"* Tonya replied. *"Kim Chow."* *"Present!"* Kim yelled out. *"Jose Hernandez."* *"Present!"* Jose replied. *"John Green."* *"Present!"* John responded. *"Kelly Johnson."* *"Present!"* Kelly replied. *"Darrell*

King." *"Present!"* Darrell replied, *"and Zoe Jones"* from the back of the class a shallow voice replied *"here."* Mrs. Jefferson responded to Zoe's response to roll call in anger screaming *"Zoe Jones were you paying attention when I asked all the students to reply to roll call by saying present?"* *"No ma'am I didn't hear you Mrs. Jefferson, I'm sorry I am present."* Mrs. Jefferson realized that there was something wrong with Zoe so she instructed the class to reply to roll call by saying here or present, she went on to say *"whichever is fine by me."*

Mrs. Jefferson began to go over the class rules with the students. *"Now class let's get down to business."* As she struck the chalk board with her four foot ruler. *"These are the rules and regulations of my classroom, they are very easy to follow and hopefully hard to break."* Mrs. Jefferson said with a smile.

*"**Rule #1:** There will be absolutely no talking during class, unless we are taking a break."*

"***Rule #2****: There will be absolutely no talking or cheating while taking a test. If this rule is broken your test grade will count as a zero.*"

"***Rule #3:*** *There will be no disrupting the classroom.*"

"***Rule #4:*** *There will be no class clowning.*"

"***Rule #5:*** *There will be absolutely no fussing or fighting, and we can all get along by showing each other respect.*"

"***Rule #6:*** *There are absolutely no TEACHER'S PETS!*"

Mrs. Jefferson went on to say *"I treat all my students the same here at W. G. Wesley Middle School. I ask that all of my students treat their peers with love and respect. I would also like for students to raise their hands if and when they have questions to ask and give me respect as well, so let's work together to make this a successful school year and the best year ever!"* Mrs. Jefferson spoke with great enthuse, the students happily yelled out *"alright Mrs. Jefferson!"*

The students took their assignments and worked quietly. Kelly whispered *"hey Zoe who would have thought that we would be in the same homeroom?"* Without looking up Zoe replied *"yeah who would have thought?"* Kelly and Zoe continued to work on their assignments. A few hours went by and the bell ranged out Ding! Ding! Ding! *"It's time for P.E."* Mrs. Jefferson yelled out, *students put your pencils down; it's time for physical education! Let's go outside, I want you all to form a straight line and no pushing."* The students followed Mrs. Jefferson to the back door of the school to the outside on the field.

"Alright students after we exercise you can all do as you please, this is your time to socialize and get to know your peers." The students began to exercise on Mrs. Jefferson's command. *"Give me ten jumping jacks, ten knee bends, ten sidekicks' ten waist twisters, and ten head shoulder, knees and toes!"* Mrs. Jefferson yelled out. The students

were so tired by the time they got to ten of the sidekicks', Mrs. Jefferson laughed and said *"alright students that's enough, you can all fall out now!"*

All the students ran out on the school yard laughing and playing. But not Zoe Jones, Zoe walked over to the swing set and began to swing alone while all of the other children ran and played. Kelly walked over and got into the other swing and began to swing alongside Zoe. There was nothing but silence and the sound of the wind blowing with each push of air from the swings, the girls kicked their legs back and forth enjoying the movement of the swings. All of a sudden Zoe asked *"hey Kelly do you live with both of your parents?"*

"Kelly replied with excitement and laughter, *"why Zoe Jones for the first time, you finally opened your mouth without someone asking you a question. No my parents are divorced my mom has a new husband and he's my step-dad, why do you ask Zoe?"* Zoe looked at Kelly with tears in her eyes and replied *"my parents are divorcing me."* Kelly began to laugh, *"What's so funny Kelly? I don't see anything to laugh about!"* Zoe replied in anger.

Kelly looked at Zoe and realized that she had offended her, Kelly immediately jumped off the swing and grab Zoe's swing, stopping it and replied *"Zoe I didn't mean to upset you it's just that parents don't divorce kids, they divorce each other."* Zoe responded *"but my parents are getting a divorced they are all I have and I don't want a step dad or a step mother ever!"* Ding! Ding! Ding! The bell rings and Mrs. Jefferson yells out *"time for lunch children!"* All the kids yelled with excitement *"yeah!"* *"No running children no running."* Mrs. Jefferson yelled out to the children as they ran into the building.

Chapter

2

After lunch the children reported to their third and fourth period class. Jose Hernandez and John Green were racing each other down the hall, *"absolutely no running in the hallway children, slow down before one of you gets hurt."* That would be the voice of Mr. Smith the Science and Social Studies teacher. *"Hello children welcome to my class, my name is Mr. Smith this class period will be your third and fourth period class because it is a combination of science and social studies."*

The children were at awe of all the many pictures of the moon and the planets that surrounded it. Tony yelled across the room *"hay Darrell look at the planet earth."* John replied sarcastically *"duh that would be where we are."* The boys begin laughing; *"Alright children quiet down for a little while I have to do role call"* Mr. Smith said to the children *"give me a minute while I get my role book out." "Mr. Smith how would you like for us to answer you when you call the roll?"* Kelly asked, Mr. Smith responded to Kelly by saying *"you can answer by either here or present it doesn't matter which one just as long as you are respectful."*

Mr. Smith began calling the role: *"Tonya Amis." "Present."* Tonya replied. *"Kim Chow." "Present!"* Kim yelled out. *"Hose Hernandez," "Present."* Hose replied. *"John Green." "Present."* John responded. *"Kelly Johnson." "Present."* Kelly replied. *"Darrell King." "Present."* Darrell replied, *"and Zoe Jones" "here Mr. Smith"* Zoe replied. The children seemed to be excited to be in Mr. Smith's class. After calling the role Mr. Smith begin passing out science and social studies books to the children. *"Okay students these are your books please keep up with them as well as take good care of them, they are to be returned at the end of the semester and if you lose your book you will have to pay for it and if your book is not returned or in the case of a lost book it has to be paid for before the end of the school year, you will not be promoted."* Mr. Smith informed the children. *"I am passing around a roster with each student's name on it, please sign your initials by your name to show proof of receiving these books."* Mr. Smith instructed the students. The children all signed the roster upon receiving their books and began to flip through the pages. Mr. Smith began to instruct the children: *"alright students I want you all to use this class period to read chapter one in your science book silently and as homework tonight I would like for you all to read chapter two and we will have in class discussion on tomorrow."* The children read silently as their class period came to an end.

Ding! Ding! Ding! The bell rang signifying that it was time for the children to change classes, *"finally fifth period"* Darrell replied. *"I take it our fifth period is Math"* Zoe replied. The children all went into the class room and took a seat, by this time they were all worn out from the classes before. Mr. Thomas the math teacher began to address the class *"hello students my name is Mr. Thomas and I will be your math teacher I will be teaching pre-algebra for this semester, I know that sometimes math can be very hard and boring, however I will make math an easy and fun subject to learn. First I will call the roll to make sure everyone assigned to this class is here."* Mr. Thomas began to call the roll: *"Tonya Amis." "Present."* Tonya replied. *"Kim Chow." "Present!"* Kim yelled out. *"Jose Hernandez." "Present."* Jose replied. *"John Green." "Present."* John responded. *"Kelly Johnson." "Present."* Kelly replied. *"Darrell King." "Present."* Darrell replied, *"and Zoe Jones,"* "here" Zoe replied. After Mr. Thomas was done calling the role Darrell yelled out with excitement *"wow we have all of our classes together this is going to be fun!"*

Mr. Thomas *looked in the back of the class and noticed that across the room Zoe had her head down on the desk,* "excuse me young lady, what is your name?" Mr. Thomas asked, *"Zoe, Zoe Jones."* "Why do you have your head on the desk Zoe? Are you alright, do you need to see the school nurse?" Mr. Thomas asked, Zoe replied in a low tone *"no Mr. Thomas I'm okay."* Mr. Thomas replied "I am going to have to ask you to take your head off of your desk and pay attention." Mr. Thomas then goes on to address the students, as he began to put math problems on the chalk board, *"In the future students if anyone is not feeling well please let me know and I will give you a pass to see the school nurse."* After Mr. Thomas *was done writing the problems on the chalk board he alerted the students,* "alright students there are twenty problems on the board, I would like for you to do problems number *one through ten right now in class and problems eleven through twenty for homework tonight."*

The students sat quietly as they worked on their math problems. *"Does anyone need help or have any questions about the problems?"* Mr. Smith asked, *"no Mr. Smith"* the students replied. Ding! Ding! Ding! The bell began to ring finally school was over and it was time for the children to go home. *"Alright students pass in your math problems one through ten and remember to do math problems eleven through twenty for homework and turn it in on tomorrow!"* Mr. Thomas shouted to the students. *"I want everyone to walk safely to your designated area to wait for the school bus or your parents to pick you up."* Mr. Smith instructed the students. The children were so happy that it was the end of the school day; they all ran out of the class without looking back or responding to Mr. Smith. Mr. Smith knew that the students were exhausted so he allowed them to run through the hallways to get to their designated pick up spot for pickup.

Chapter

3

Zoe's mother was looking out of the kitchen window when Zoe's school bus arrived; she met Zoe at the door. *"Hi Zoe how was your first day of middle school?"* Zoe continued to walk pass her mother as she responded in a low toned voice *"it was fine I like it okay."* Zoe continued walking into her bedroom and closed the door behind her; Zoe's mother approached Zoe's room and began knocking on the door, *"Zoe, Zoe, what's the matter Zoe?"* Zoe did not respond to her mother's knock so her mother went into the room and sat on Zoe's bed *"what's the matter Zoe? Why didn't you answer me when I knocked on your door?"* As the sound of sniffles began to get louder Zoe's mother realized that Zoe was crying.

"Zoe what's wrong why are you crying?" Her mother asked, Zoe responded *"because you and dad are divorcing me"*, *"Zoe we are not divorcing you, where did you get that idea?"* Her mother replied, Zoe looked up at her mother and began to cry even harder, responding *"I heard you and dad talking and I know that you are breaking up I know that you are getting a divorce."* Zoe's mother looked at Zoe and said *"Zoe we didn't want to tell you right away because you were starting middle school and we did not want this to interfere with you and school, we really want you to have the best school year ever, however your dad and I do not see eye to eye and it's just not working out with us."*

Zoe responded to her mother *"but what about me, why are you doing this to me, don't you guys love me?"* Zoe's mother responded *"of course we love you Zoe and don't you ever think differently, just because your dad and I are getting a divorce does not mean that we don't love you, we will still be here for you, however your dad will be living in a separate place he will still be in your life. You will spend some weekends and holidays with your dad however you will live here with me."* Zoe's mother wiped the tears from Zoe's eyes and pulled her by the hand saying *"now come on Zoe and eat your dinner."* Zoe went into the bathroom and washed her face, and then she went into the dining room to eat her dinner.

Zoe sat down at the table but she did not eat a bite of her food, her mother did not press her to eat she just watched as Zoe laid her head on the dining room table and fell asleep. After she finished eating her dinner Zoe's mother woke Zoe up and instructed her to take a bath and get in the bed. The next school day Zoe did not do well in school she cried throughout all of her classes and when it was time for math Mr. Thomas sent Zoe to see Ms. Cramer, the school nurse. When Zoe arrived to the nursing office with her pass Ms. Cramer asked *"what's wrong Zoe, are you hurting anywhere Zoe?"* Zoe responded *"no ma'am, I'm not hurting anywhere, I am sad because my parents are divorcing me."* *"Oh okay, I see this is not a school nurse problem, this is a school counselor's issue, let me take you to see Ms. Harrison the school counselor Zoe."* *"Okay"* Zoe replied.

Knock! Knock! Knock! The sound of Ms. Cramer knocking on the school counselor's door, *"come in"* Ms. Harrison responded *"Hello Ms. Harrison"* Ms. Cramer spoke as she held Zoe by the hand, walking her into the office *"hello Ms. Cramer, whom do we have here?"* Ms. Harrison responded. *This is Zoe Jones and there's something bothering her, that I felt only you could help her with, so I will leave you two alone to discuss them and when you are done with Zoe if you would please give her a pass back to class to let her teacher;*

Mr. Thomas know that she was with you." "Sure I can do that; in fact I will walk her back to class myself." *"Thanks that would be even better."* Ms. Cramer replied, *"You are more than welcomed"* Ms. Harrison responded.

Ms. Harrison stood up from her desk and walked Ms. Cramer to the door and closed it behind her. *"Okay Zoe let me introduce myself; I am Ms. Harrison the school counselor and I want you to know that you can talk to me about whatever you feel comfortable talking about and I can assure you that what you discuss with me will not be discussed with anyone else outside of this office unless I feel that there is something I need to discuss with your parents because of you being a minor, is that understood?"* Nodding her head Zoe responded *"yes ma'am I understand."* *"So what seems to be the problem Zoe?"* Ms. Harrison asked. *"I have trouble paying attention in class, I feel sad and I cry all the time."* Zoe responded as she rubbed her hands together and played with her fingers.

"How long has this been going on Zoe?" Ms. Harrison asked, *"Well I've been crying and feeling sad for about two weeks before school started and I have not been able to pay attention since school started"* Zoe replied. Ms. Harrison took notes as Zoe talked then she responded *"can you tell me what brought these feelings on Zoe?"* Zoe began to disclose to Ms. Harrison *"before school started back I heard my mom and dad saying that they were getting as a divorce and my dad hasn't been living at home since."* Zoe replied, *"How does that make you feel Zoe?"* Ms. Harrison inquired. *"I feel really bad because I don't know what I did to make them divorce me, I try to be a good child I mean I wash the dishes, I clean my room and I do whatever my parents ask me to do, so I don't know what I have done to make my parents' divorce me!"* Zoe responded raising her voice as tears ran from her eyes. *"It's okay Zoe, it's okay"* Ms. Harrison replied to Zoe.

Ms. Harrison laid her pad and pen on the desk and responded *"so what I hear you saying* is that you're upset because you think that you are the reason your parents are getting a divorce, and you feel bad because they are doing so, am I right Zoe?" *'Yes ma'am"* Zoe responded. Ms. Harrison responded *"Zoe is it alright if I call your mother to discuss what you've discussed with me so that we can get your questions answered?"* *"Yes ma'am that's fine you can call my mother, her name is Mrs. Taylor Jones and her phone number is 404-838-0928."* Zoe replied. *"Well Zoe if that's all we are done and I will take you back to class."* Zoe replied *"thank you Ms. Harrison and thank you for listening."* As she and Ms. Harrison walked out of the office. Mr. Harrison took Zoe back to class and returned to her office to call Zoe's mother.

Chapter

4

Ring! Ring! Ring! The telephone rang as Ms. Harrison attempted to get Zoe's mother on the telephone. *"Hello"* Zoe's mother responded as she answered the telephone, *good afternoon may I speak with Mrs. Taylor Jones"* Ms. Harrison responded, *"this is Taylor Jones, whom am I speaking with?"* Mrs. Jones replied. *"Mrs. Jones this is the school counselor here at Wesley Middle School"* *"hi, what's going on is Zoe okay?"* Mrs.

Jones asked. *"No Zoe is fine there's just some concerns I have with her if you could come to the school a little bit early, right before Zoe gets out of her last class today, so that we may talk here in my office and I will be able to share those concerns with you."* Ms. Harrison replied. *"Sure that will be fine Ms. Harrison I will see you at two-thirty and thanks for calling."* Mrs. Jones replied, Ms. Harrison responded, *"you are welcomed and I will see you soon goodbye."*

Mrs. Jones arrived at the school, as she walked into the building she stopped at the receptionist desk. *"Hello, how may I help you?"* the receptionist replied, *"Hello I am Mrs. Taylor Jones and I have a meeting at two-thirty with Ms. Harrison the school counselor"* the receptionist picked up the phone and called into Ms. Harrison's office *"Ms. Harrison, Mrs. Jones is here to see you"* *"okay, I will come out to get her"* Ms. Harrison replied. *"You may have a seat and Ms. Harrison will be right out to get you Mrs. Jones"* the receptionist replied. Click! Click! Click! As her heels touched the marble floor, Ms. Harris stepped up to the receptionist desk reaching for Mrs. Jones hand to shake and said *"hello Mrs. Jones, I am Ms. Harrison you may come right in and have a seat."* Mrs. Jones walked into the office and took a seat and waited for Ms. Harrison to sit down, as she sat down at her desk she responded *"Mrs. Jones the reason I called this meeting with you today is because Zoe was brought into my office by Ms. Cramer our school Nurse, it seems Zoe has been having difficulties paying attention in all of her classes and she seems to have had some crying outburst in class as well."* Mrs. Jones listened quietly as Ms. Harrison continued to talk, *"when I asked Zoe what was going on she responded by saying quote unquote "my parents are divorcing me." Zoe seems to think that she is the cause of the divorce and she would like to know what she has done so badly to cause her parents to get a divorce."* Mrs. Jones responded with a long breath *"it's true my husband and I are getting a divorce, however Zoe has nothing to do with us deciding to get a divorce, Zoe is a great child, she's as sweet as she could be, she's the love of our lives and I feel really bad that she thinks that she is the cause of our separation because she is not."* Mrs. Jones goes on to say *"Zoe and I had a long talk about the situation and I explained to her that her father and I love her very much and will continue to love her even after the divorce is final, I don't know what else I can to do to reassure Zoe that she is not the problem."*

Ms. Harrison opened up her file cabinet and pulled out a folder replying *"Mrs. Jones I called you into to discuss this problem and to make sure you were aware of how your divorce is affecting Zoe as well as her performance in school, in hopes that you and your husband will get Zoe some help to deal with her feelings so that this situation may not affect her in the future."* *"Some help? What type of help are you speaking of?"* Mrs. Jones responded, opening up the folder Ms. Harrison replied *"Mrs. Jones I have a list of therapists and counselors who specializes in marriage and family that you may seek counseling from, if you would like to call one of them to set up* an appointment, you can do so at your convenience." Ms. Harrison goes on to say "I also think that it would be a good idea for the entire family to attend the session for family counseling." Ding! Ding! Ding! The bell rang. Ms. Harrison handed Mrs. Jones the list of therapists and counselors and shook her hand responding *"that's the bell ringing and school is over, Zoe will be waiting for you outside, thank you for coming Mrs. Jones."* as Mrs. Jones exited the office she replied *"thank you very much for calling me and having me to come in to discuss this matter, and thank you for the referral I will get this taken care of as soon as possible."*

As Mrs. Jones walked out of Ms. Harrison office the hallways were full of children running down the hall as she walked toward the front door Zoe came running out of nowhere *"hi mom, what are you doing here?"* Zoe asked, as Mrs. Jones and Zoe walked out of the building Mrs. Jones wrapped her arms around Zoe's shoulders and continued silently to the car, once they were in the car, Mrs. Jones responded *"I had a meeting with Ms. Harrison, the school counselor and Zoe I did not know that this divorce was affecting you at home as well as in school, but I want you to know that your father and I love you very much no matter what happens."* Mrs. Jones goes on to say *"just because your father and I are getting a divorce, does not mean that we are divorcing you, although your father will not be living in the same home with you, Zoe you can always visit his home, spend the weekends and take summer vacations with him, Zoe whenever you want to visit your father it's alright with me."* Zoe responded *"I know you and dad love me, I'm just scared that when you get the divorce he will get a new wife, have more children and forget all about me."* *"No Zoe your father will never forget about you he loves you very much, you're his daughter and the love of his life."* Mrs. Jones replied.

Upon arriving home Mrs. Jones unlocked the front door and she and Zoe entered the house *"Zoe do you have any home work?"* Mrs. Jones asked *"No mom"* Zoe replied. Zoe went in her bedroom and started to watch television, Mrs. Jones went into her bedroom to put her things down, she flopped down on her bed and let out a big sigh, then picked up the telephone calling Zoe's father.

Chapter

5

Ring! Ring! Ring! The telephone rang as Zoe's mother attempted to call her husband. *"Hello"* Mr. Jones answered, *"hello Tom it's Taylor"* Mrs. Jones responded. *"Hello Taylor, how are you? Is everything alright with you and Zoe?"* Mr. Jones inquired. Rubbing her head Mrs. Jones replied *"Tom, Zoe isn't dealing with this divorce to well; she seems to think that she is the reason we are getting a divorce and not only that, she thinks that we are divorcing her as well."* Mr. Jones listened carefully as Mrs. Jones talked, *"It seems that Zoe was having problems at school so her teacher sent her to talk with the school counselor and during their discussion Zoe revealed that every since she found out about the divorce she has been crying and feeling sad and now that school has started she's having trouble paying attention in class because all she can think about is us getting a divorce."*

Mr. Jones replied *"wow I did not know that us getting a divorce was affecting Zoe that bad, so what do we do?"* Mr. Jones inquired, Mrs. Jones responded *"well Tom although I have talked to Zoe about the situation and reassured her that we love her no matter what happens."* Mrs. Jones goes on to say *"I would like for you to talk with Zoe as well."* *"Alright I will talk with Zoe right now, will you call her to the phone?"* Mr. Jones asked, *"Sure I will call her to the phone, oh and Tom there's one other thing,"* Mrs. Jones replied, *"What's that Taylor?"* Mr. Jones asked *"the school counselor thought it would be a good idea for us as a family to speak with a marriage and family therapist to help Zoe deal with the divorce a little bit better."* Mrs. Jones replied, *"that's fine with me Taylor when do we go?"* Mr. Jones asked *"*tomorrow at twelve noon and Zoe will miss school so that she may attend the session as well." Mrs. Jones *replied "well then tomorrow it is, now may I speak to my little princess?" Mr. Jones asked.* As she called Zoe to the phone Mrs. Jones replied *"thanks Tom, Zoe your dad is on the telephone and he would like to speak with you for a moment." Zoe ran excitedly to the telephone.*

"Hello dad, how are you today?" Zoe asked, Mr. Jones replied *"Hi Zoe, I'm fine princess, what about you?"* Zoe responded *"I'm okay dad."* Mr. Jones responded *"Zoe your mother tells me that you have been having trouble dealing with the thought of us getting a divorce and I hear it's affecting you in school."* *"Well dad I feel sad because I don't know what I did to make you and mom break up, I mean I do my best and I do everything that you and mom ask me to do, I just don't know why you*

guys are divorcing me." Mr. Jones responded *"Zoe I want you to know that your mother and I love you very much and there is nothing you did to make us decide to get a divorce, I want you to know that your mother and I love each other very much, there's just some things we don't see eye to eye on and we don't want to raise you in a home with a lot of arguing and bickering, you are not the reason we are getting a divorce and we are not divorcing you."* Mr. Jones goes on to say *"although I won't live in the same home with you and your mother, I will continue to be in your life and most importantly your mother and I will always love you no matter what."* *"I know dad, mom told me, I'm going to bed now, I love you dad, goodbye."* Zoe responded, *"I love you too princess."* Mr. Jones replied and ended the phone call.

Zoe and Mr. Jones both hung up the telephone, Zoe kneeled down by her bed and folded her hands together and began to pray, *"now I lay me down to sleep I pray the lord my soul to keep and If I should die before I awake I pray the lord my soul to take, Lord bless me, my mom, my dad, all of my family, my classmates, my teachers, Mr. Pringly and especially Ms. Harrison for listening to me and trying to help my parents out. Lord please don't let my parent's divorce me, I haven't done anything wrong, I love my parents and I would do anything for them to stay together, if not Lord please help me through this divorce amen."* After praying Zoe got into bed pulled the covers over her head and began to cry until she fell asleep.

Chapter

6

The next morning came and the house was quiet, Zoe was in her room getting dressed and Mrs. Jones was in the bathroom combing her hair, suddenly there was a knock on the door. Knock! Knock! Knock! *"Who is it?"* Mrs. Jones asked *"Taylor it's me Tom."* Mr. Jones responded, excitedly Zoe ran to the door and opened it as Mr. Jones entered the house Zoe jumped into his arms, *"hi dad."* Zoe said excitedly with a smile as bright as the *sun,* as he swung Zoe around in the air Mr. Smith responded *"hello my little princess, hello Taylor, is everyone all set to go?"* Grabbing her purse and handing Mr. Jones the directions to the therapist's office, Mrs. Jones responded *"hi Tom, yes we are all set to go, come on Zoe we don't want to be late."*

As they were on their way to see the marriage and family therapist, there was an awkward silence in the car, Mr. Jones looked straight ahead as he drove, Mrs. Jones gazed out of the passenger side window and Zoe laid in the back seat until she fell off to sleep. Mr. Jones drove for a while, then finally they arrive at the therapist office, *"were here Zoe wake up were here."* Mr. Jones called out; Mrs. Jones looked back at Zoe and said wake up Zoe were here. Mr. Jones got out of the car and walked over to the passenger side to open the door for Mrs. Jones then he opened the back door for Zoe to get out of the car, at the same time Mrs. Jones and Zoe replied *"thank you."*

They all walked into the front office, Mrs. Jones walked up to the receptionist window and said *"hello we are the Jones's and we have an appointment for twelve noon."* *"Okay Mrs. Jones if you would please sign the clip board and I will let the therapist know that you all are her."* The receptionist responded, *"thank you"* Mrs. Jones replied. The receptionist picked up the phone and said *"Ms. Whitt your twelve noon appointment is here."* *"Okay I will be right out."* The therapist replied. Suddenly the door opened to the back office *"Hello, I'm Ms. Whitt and you must be the Jones's?"* The therapist replied, and all at once the Jones's replied *"hello."* The therapist motioned her hand saying *"follow me to my office please."* The Jones followed Ms. Whitt to her office; once they were in the office Ms. Whitt replied *"you may all have a seat,"* The Jones sat down and waited for the therapist to speak.

The therapist took out a pad and pen to take notes, once she had gotten settled in at her desk she began to address the Jones. *"As I said before I am Ms. Whitt I will be your marriage and family therapist for today."* As she continued to speak she asked *"what brings you in today?"* Mrs. Jones responded *"I'm Mrs. Jones,"* pointing her finger at Mr. Jones and Zoe she continued to introduce them *"this is my husband Tom and this is our daughter Zoe."* Mrs. Jones continued to speak *"we were referred here by a school counselor at Zoe's school."* Mrs. Jones goes on to say *"you see my husband and I are getting a divorce and not only does Zoe seem to think that she's the reason we are getting a divorce, she thinks we are divorcing her as well and as a result, it's affecting Zoe in school as well as at home."* Nodding her head Ms. Whitt responded *"so what I hear you saying is that you and Mr. Jones are going through a divorce, Zoe seems to think she's the cause of it and as a result it's affecting her emotionally."* Mr. and Mrs. Jones responded *"yes, that's right."*

"First of all let me say that I am pleased that the school counselor provided you with the referral for a marriage and family therapist, because it's important

that you seek counseling from an individual that specializes in the marriage and family area, and I say that because when assessing the problem I focus on the distress and dynamics that have a negative impact within the family system as well as helping families to develop positive interpersonal skills to deal with the targeted issues. "The Jones's listened carefully as Ms. Whitt continued to talk, *"what I'm going to do is allow each of you a chance to talk so that we may find a solution to this problem."* The session went on for one hour and once it was over Ms. Whitt gave the Jones an appointment to return one month from their initial visit.

The Jones left the center and headed home, on the way home Zoe talked about what she had learned in the counseling session. Zoe put one arm around the driver seat and one arm around the passenger seat and gave her parents a hug, as she hugged them she responded *"mom, dad I learned that just because you guys are getting a divorce does not mean that you don't love me, it doesn't mean that you don't love each other and it does not mean that you are divorcing me." Zoe goes on to say "I think that if two parents aren't getting alone and there is a child in the home then the parents should get a divorce because all of the fussing and the fighting will only make the child as well as the home unhappy and I don't want to be unhappy."* Zoe's parents both replied at the same time well that's true Zoe and I'm glad you understand it now.

The next day Zoe returned to school, it was a better day for her because she no longer thought that her parents were divorcing her. In every class Zoe attended she paid attention, laughed and smiled all day long. As the school year went by Zoe did well, her parent's divorce was finalize and Mr. and Mrs. Jones shared custody of Zoe. The Jones learned how to communicate more effectively and positively, and they learned that whenever they had any disagreements, that they were not to involve or use Zoe as ammunition or leverage against each other because it would only affect her more. The Jones learned to get along for

Zoe's sake and Zoe got through the school year happier than ever.

The End

Africa Hann © 2013

Printed in the United States
By Bookmasters